D0783679

Margaret Tempest.

SQUIRREL GOES SKATING

BY ALISON UTTLEY

PICTURES BY MARGARET TEMPEST

Collins

First published in Great Britain by
William Collins Sons & Co in 1934
This edition published by
HarperCollins Publishers Ltd in 1993
Text copyright © The Alison Uttley
Literary Property Trust 1986
Illustrations copyright
© The Estate of Margaret Tempest 1986
Copyright this arrangement
© William Collins Sons & Co Ltd 1986

Illustration on p. 4 by Mary Cooper
Alison Uttley's original story
has been abridged for this book.

A CIP catalogue record for this title
is available from the British Library.

ISBN: 0 00 194220 4

Printed and bound in Italy

This book is set in Goudy

Collins

An Imprint of HarperCollins*Publishers*

FOREWORD

Of course you must understand that Grey Rabbit's home had no electric light or gas, and even the candles were made from pith of rushes dipped in wax from the wild bees' nests, which Squirrel found. Water there was in plenty, but it did not come from a tap. It flowed from a spring outside, which rose up from the ground and went to a brook. Grey Rabbit cooked on a fire, but it was a wood fire, there was no coal in that part of the country. Tea did not come from India, but from a little herb known very well to country people, who once dried it and used it in their cottage homes. Bread was baked from wheat ears, ground fine, and Hare and Grey Rabbit gleaned in the cornfields to get the wheat.

The doormats were plaited rushes, like country-made mats, and cushions were stuffed with wool gathered from the hedges where sheep pushed through the thorns. As for the looking-glass, Grey Rabbit found the glass, dropped from a lady's handbag, and Mole made a frame for it. Usually the animals gazed at themselves in the still pools as so many country children have done. The country ways of Grey Rabbit were the country ways known to the author.

Everything was frozen. Even the brook, which ran past little Grey Rabbit's house on the edge of the wood, was thick with ice. Each blade of grass had a white fringe, and the black, leafless trees were patterned with shining crystals.

On every window of the house were Jack Frost's pictures – trees and ferns and flowers in silver.

Little Grey Rabbit stood looking at them, when Hare came downstairs in his brown dressing-gown.

"Grey Rabbit! Grey Rabbit!" he called. "Put some more wood on the fire. It's bitter cold today."

Grey Rabbit left the window and put a log on the fire.

"I believe I've got a chilblain," said Hare in a complaining voice. "Yes I thought so. It's a big chilblain! What can you do for it, Grey Rabbit?"

Grey Rabbit went to the medicine cupboard and looked at the bottles which stood in a row.

There was Primrose wine for coughs and colds and feast days. There was Dandelion for toothache, and Dock leaves for bruises, St. John's Wort for cuts, but nothing for chilblains.

"There isn't anything for chilblains," said Grey Rabbit, sadly.

"Ow! Ow!" exclaimed Hare, rubbing his toe. "Do think of something, Grey Rabbit. You don't know how it hurts!"

"Moldy Warp once told me to use snow," said Grey Rabbit. "I'll get some."

She ran outside and scraped the rime from the grass. Then she rubbed Hare's foot till the chilblain disappeared.

"Grey Rabbit! Grey Rabbit!" called Squirrel, coming downstairs with a shawl over her shoulders. "Pile up the fire and keep out the cold. You've had the door open this frosty morning."

So Grey Rabbit put another log on the fire, and sent away the little wind which had rushed in when she went out.

At last they sat down to breakfast, with hot tea and thick buttered toast.

"Milk-o," called a voice, and Hedgehog knocked at the door.

"It's fruz today," said he, as he turned a solid lump of milk out of his can.

"I went to the cow-house – it's the only really warm place on a day like this – but icicles hung all round my little door, and nearly stabbed me as I went in."

He was indeed a strange sight, with his prickles all frost covered.

"Come in and warm yourself," said Grey Rabbit.

He stamped his feet at the door and tiptoed over to the fire. Grey Rabbit gave him a cup of tea. And as he sipped from the saucer, he talked.

"There's skating over Tom Tiddler's Way, and I've heard tell everyone is going," he said.

"Moldy Warp was trying on his skates as I came past, and I met a couple of brown rabbits with their toboggan."

Hare put down his cup.

"Let's go too," said he. "Hurry up everybody," and he gobbled up his breakfast as fast as he could.

"There's no hurry, Mr Hare," drawled Hedgehog. "Ice'll wait. There'll be no thaw this side Christmas, I can tell 'ee that." And he took another sip of his tea.

"Well, I must be getting on," he said, wiping his mouth with his red handkerchief. And he tiptoed out again, leaving a little stream on the floor. Grey Rabbit wiped it away.

Hare jumped up from the table. "Have you ever seen me skate?" he asked. "I'm a very good skater. Did you ever hear how I skated round the Lily Pond backwards? I'll tell you about it."

"Not now," said Grey Rabbit. "We must get our skates cleaned, and the house tidied and the lunch ready."

"And put on our best clothes," added Squirrel.

Hare went out to clean the skates, Squirrel disappeared upstairs, and Grey Rabbit did everything else as quickly as she could. She swept the floor, made up the fire, cut the sandwiches and packed them in the basket. She even remembered to put in an extra loaf for any hungry rooks who might be on the ice.

When she stood ready to go, with a little red muffler round her neck, she called Hare and Squirrel.

"Hare, are you ready? Hare?"

Hare came running with a basket of icicles. "I've been collecting these to take for drinks," he said. "You just suck one like this."

"That's splendid," said Grey Rabbit, "but I think we should take the kettle too, for hot drinks."

"And a lemon," added Hare, "for hot lemonade."

"But you haven't changed your dressing-gown," said Grey Rabbit. "And where are the skates?"

"Oh, Jemima!" exclaimed Hare. "I forgot the skates and my dressing-gown."

He hurried off to get ready.

"Squirrel! Squirrel! Are you ready? We're going," called Grey Rabbit at the foot of the stairs.

"Coming," called Squirrel, and Grey Rabbit took a look round. The table was laid for their return, when they would be tired and hungry. There was herb-pie, an apple tart, and cob-nut cutlets. "I'll put out a bottle of Primrose wine," she said, going to the larder.

"Can you come here?" called Squirrel in a muffled voice. Grey Rabbit and Hare both hurried upstairs. In Squirrel's room a green dress was jumping about with two little paws waving in the air. A green-beribboned tail stuck half out of the neck of the dress, and Squirrel's head couldn't find a way out at all.

Hare and Grey Rabbit sank down on the bed, helpless with laughter. When at last they straightened her out they found Squirrel had decked herself with green bows and hung a locket round her neck.

Off they went at last, Grey Rabbit carrying the basket of food, Hare swinging the basket of icicles in one paw and the kettle in the other, and Squirrel following with the skates dangling on her arm.

They locked the door and put the key on the window-sill. Over it they sprinkled leaves and grass and a few icicles.

Then the three animals ran down the lane and across the fields towards Tom Tiddler's Way.

Little hurrying footsteps came along a side path, and a party of brown rabbits, each with a pair of skates hanging on his back, joined them.

Hare led the way, past Moldy Warp's house, and through the fields where Grey Rabbit had picked primroses for wine in the spring.

"Stop a minute," called a voice as they crossed a frozen stream and a handsome Water-rat joined them.

At last they reached the pond, which lay in the centre of a small field. Already many animals were on the ice, and the air was filled with merry cries. The newcomers sat down and put on their skates. Grey Rabbit placed her basket of food in the care of Mrs Hedgehog, who sat on a log, watching her son, Fuzzypeg.

Soon they were laughing and shouting with the others, as they skimmed over the ice.

Hare tried to do the outside edge, and got mixed up with the skates of a white duck. He fell down with a thump and bruised his forehead.

"Grey Rabbit! Grey Rabbit!" he called. "Grey Rabbit! I've bumped myself." And Grey Rabbit ran up and rubbed him with her paw. She dusted the powdered snow off his coat, and helped him to his unsteady feet. Then she went to some young brown rabbits who were in difficulties. Every time they started off, one of them sat down, and tumbled into the others, so that they were a continual bunch of kicking legs.

Grey Rabbit and Water-rat linked paws with them and steered them across the pond, to their joy and happiness. Away they went, ears back, heads up, fur stiff in the wind, their eyes shining and their breath coming and going in little puffs, as their tiny feet glided over the ice.

"I'm hungry," called Hare. "Let's have lunch." So they returned to Mrs Hedgehog, who still sat with her eyes on young Fuzzypeg and on no one else. Grey Rabbit unpacked the basket, and Squirrel invited Water-rat, Moldy Warp, Mrs Hedgehog and Fuzzypeg to join them.

There was enough for all, and still there was a loaf left for the hungry black-coated rooks who loitered on the pond's edge.

Hare's icicles were very thin by now, but he handed round the basket and each sucked the sweet cold ice. The rooks collected sticks for a fire, and soon Grey Rabbit had a kettle boiling and hot drinks of lemonade for all the company.

"Sour! Sour!" grimaced little Fuzzypeg, but his mother nudged him to remember his company manners.

They all returned to the ice and skated until the red sun set behind the hills. Dark shadows spread across the fields as the animals removed their skates and set off home.

"It *has* been a jolly day," said Grey Rabbit to Water-rat and Moldy Warp. "Good-bye. Perhaps we will come again tomorrow."

"Goodnight. Goodnight," resounded round the pond.

"Did you see me skate?" asked Hare, excitedly. "I did the double-outside-edge backwards."

"I saw all the little rabbits and fieldmice you knocked down," said Squirrel severely.

"Hush!" said Grey Rabbit. "Don't make a noise. Wise Owl doesn't like it."

The key was on the window-sill under the pile of grass but there were footprints in the garden.

"Someone's been here whilst we've been skating," said Squirrel, looking anxiously up and down.

They all hurried inside and stared in dismay. On the table lay the remains of the feast, only dirty dishes, and crusts, and an empty bottle of Primrose wine.

"Oh! Oh!" cried Hare. "I was so hungry."

"Oh! Oh!" cried Squirrel. "I was so thirsty."

"Oh! Oh!" cried Grey Rabbit. "I left such a feast and now look at it."

"Who's been here since we've been gone?" they said, running to the larder.

Not a scrap of food remained. Everything was gone and all over the floor were footprints.

They ran upstairs to the bedrooms, each carrying a candlestick.

"There's no one in my attic," whispered Grey Rabbit, as she peeped in.

"And there's no one in my room," said Hare, picking up his dressing-gown from the floor where he had flung it.

"Oo-Oo-Oo," squeaked Squirrel. "Somebody's sleeping in *my* bed! Oo-Oo-Oo."

They peered through the door, but all they could see was a long thin tail hanging down on the floor, and long black whiskers sticking out of the sheets.

"Who is it?" whispered Squirrel in a trembling voice.

"It's Rat's tail," said Hare.

"They're Rat's whiskers," said Grey Rabbit, below her breath.

"Then it must be Rat himself," sobbed Squirrel.

They tiptoed downstairs, each with a candle dropping tallow on the steps, they were so alarmed.

"What shall we do?" they asked each other as they stood in the untidy kitchen.

Hare trembled so much that the candle fell out and burnt his paws.

Squirrel forgot to use her handkerchief in her agitation and wiped her streaming eyes on her beribboned tail.

Grey Rabbit shivered as she thought of Rat's sharp teeth. But no sound came from the bedroom except snores.

"He must get out of my bed," said Squirrel. "We must shoo him out."

"But he ought to be punished," said Grey Rabbit. "We ought to make him remember his wickedness."

"When I want to remember anything I tie a knot in my handkerchief," said Hare.

Then Squirrel spoke these astonishing words. "I can tie knots," said she. "I will tie a knot in Rat's tail, and it will never, never come undone. Then he will never, never forget his wickedness."

Squirrel crept upstairs again, and Hare and Grey Rabbit followed with a candle to light her in her task.

Squirrel picked up the long tail and tied it and twisted it and turned it, and doubled it and looped it till it made one great knot, and Rat never awoke, for he had eaten and drunk so much from little Grey Rabbit's larder.

They shut the door and ran downstairs, with beating hearts.

"Now we must frighten him away," said Grey Rabbit.

Hare took the tongs and poker, Grey Rabbit took two saucepan lids, and Squirrel took the bundle of skates. They hammered and banged against the bedroom door and made such a clang and clatter, such a rattle and racket that the Rat awoke.

He sprang out of bed, opened the window and jumped out.

"Whatever's that a-bumping and a-clumping behind me?" said he to himself, and he turned round to find his tail in a knot.

He ran down the paths with the knot reminding him of his wickedness all the way, and he didn't like it at all.

At last he sat down and tried to undo the knot, but just then Wise Owl came sailing along the sky. He spied Rat down below, trying to unfasten his tail.

"Hello, Rat!" said he, and he flew down to look. "Hello! Been in mischief?" He chuckled in a goblin way, which made Rat shiver, then flew soundlessly away.

In the little house Grey Rabbit put clean sheets on Squirrel's bed, Squirrel swept the floor and Hare made a fire in the kitchen to cheer everybody up as there was no food.

Suddenly there came a knock at the door. Thump! thump! thump!

The three animals looked at one another anxiously.

"Grey Rabbit! Open the door," cried a voice.

"That's Mole," said Grey Rabbit, and she flung wide the door.

"We are so glad to see you," she cried, as Mole staggered in with a big hamper, followed by Water-rat with another.

They opened the baskets and took out eggs, sandwiches, tea-cakes, a Bakewell tart, and a big plum-cake with icing.

"Hurrah!" cried the three, dancing round the room.

"Hedgehog is bringing an extra can of milk," said Mole. "I thought you might be short."

"It's still fruz," said Old Hedgehog, putting the milk on the table.

"Come along, Hedgehog, and join the party," they cried, and he sat down on the settle, keeping his prickles to himself.

After supper they sang songs, ending up with, "He's a jolly good fellow," and toasted Mole and Water-rat in a bottle of Primrose wine which the Rat had overlooked.

Then Mole and Water-rat said goodbye, and walked along the quiet field paths to their homes.